For more than forty years,
Yearling has been the leading name
in classic and award-winning literature
for young readers.

Yearling books feature children's
favorite authors and characters,
providing dynamic stories of adventure,
humor, history, mystery, and fantasy.

Trust Yearling paperbacks to entertain,
inspire, and promote the love of reading
in all children.

THE FUTURE IS NOW!

Read all the Time Surfers books:

SPACE BINGO

ORBIT WIPEOUT!

MONDO MELTDOWN

INTO THE ZONK ZONE!

SPLASH CRASH!

ZERO HOUR

SHOCK WAVE

DOOM STAR

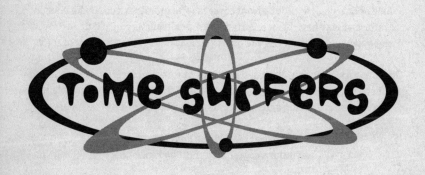

DOOM STAR

ILLUSTRATED BY KIM MULKEY

A YEARLING BOOK

Published by Yearling, an imprint of Random House Children's Books
a division of Random House, Inc., New York

This is a work of fiction. Names, characters, places, and incidents either are the
product of the author's imagination or are used fictitiously. Any resemblance to
actual persons, living or dead, events, or locales is entirely coincidental.

Text copyright © 1997 by Robert T. Abbott
Illustrations copyright © 1997 by Kim Mulkey

Visit us on the Web! www.randomhouse.com/kids

Educators and librarians, for a variety of teaching tools,
visit us at www.randomhouse.com/teachers

ISBN: 978-0-553-48465-6
Printed in the United States of America
Originally published by Bantam Skylark in 1997
First Yearling Edition January 2009
11 10 9 8 7 6 5 4 3 2

Random House Children's Books supports the First Amendment
and celebrates the right to read.

For my brother Rick,
creator of Kortak
and his antimolecular ray

CHAPTER
* 1 *

Zzzz! Kkk! Jjjjt!

The sizzling fiery ball spat sparks in all directions as it shot through the air after Ned Banks.

He ducked and skittered back across the slick metal floor, struggling to escape.

"Got to get to the stairs!" his best friend, Ernie Somers, yelled out from somewhere above him.

Ned scanned the shimmering steps. "Yes!" Leap up the steps to the next level of this crazy maze of shadows and light. Escape!

But—*kkk! zzzz!*—the ball zoomed to the top of the stairs first, sparking faster than before.

Uh-oh. Things had just gone into hyperdrive.

"Reverse! Reverse!" Ernie cried to his friend.

Yes, that was the only way. Ned had to spin on his heels and jump back to where he'd come from. Do everything in reverse order.

Ned whirled instantly, a blur of movement.

But the floor below was now a swirling dark sea, shooting flashes of electricity like a snake spitting poison.

"The vortex! I'm doomed!" Ned cried out.

WHOOSH! The dark air reached up with powerful fingers and pulled him down. Everything went black. Ned withered. His atoms spun away in a million directions. He searched for Ernie's face, snap-waved, closed his eyes, and faded.

Ned Banks was no more.

"Oops!" said Ernie.

"Oops?" Ned Banks looked over his friend's shoulder at the tiny 3-D figure of himself fading on the gamespace in front of them. "You get me totally zapped, and all you can say is *oops*?"

"It's only my first time," Ernie reminded Ned, setting down his control pad. "I flew into reverse when I saw the vortex. But I ran out of time."

Suzi Naguchi and Roop Johnson, the other members of Time Surfer Squad One, smiled.

"It's just a digital projection of you, Ned," Suzi said.

"I guess," Ned said. "But it still hurts."

The three-dimensional gamespace was set up on a large table in the cafeteria of *Tempus 5*, a mach-speed time freighter cruising to the faraway Omega Sector.

"Holobloogball is truly strange, Ned," Ernie said. "Miniature replicas of you and me, running around this tiny world. And you invented it."

"Tell me about it," Ned replied. "Here we are in the year 2099, playing the three-D miniversion of a game I invented in 2024, when I was grown up, seventy-five years before now, which is about a hundred years in the future from our present!"

Roop laughed and slapped Ned on the shoulder. "Time can bagel your brain, Neddo." Then he stepped over to a row of electron cookers on the galley wall, put several foil-wrapped snacks into one, and hit a switch.

At the same time—*whoosh!* A bulkhead slid up and Commander Naguchi, Suzi's father, entered the galley. He had an array of medals on the shoulders of his flight suit, and greeted the four

Surfers with an official snap wave. "We are entering Quadrant R of Omega Sector."

Ernie tapped a button on the hologame and it collapsed into a small, flat cartridge. He gave it to Ned, who slipped it into his pocket.

"Quadrant R," said Suzi, stepping over to her father. "Where the strange reports came from."

"That's right," the commander said. "In the past few days, three ships have returned to Spider Base with reports of *lost time*."

"Lost time?" Ned repeated.

Roop shook his head. "Really weird, guys. The ships are cruising on their missions, everything's normal, then—*zap!*—it's suddenly two hours later and a bunch of stuff is missing."

Ned chewed his lip. "Missing? Like what?"

"Shield lasers," Suzi said. "And buffer guns and stunners. Mostly defense weapons, but some computers, too, and—"

"Food!" said Roop, talking over his shoulder as he checked the progress of the cooker. "Food disappears from their plates. It vanishes from cupboards and freezers. And when time switches back on again, the whole ship is out of eats!"

"That's rough," Ernie mumbled as the electron cooker whirred. The smell of warm snacks was beginning to fill the room.

"As far as we can determine," Commander Naguchi went on, pacing around the large center table, "some kind of time warp event is occurring in this sector. So far, no one has seen who, or what, is behind it. Our job is to find out. But I must say, it is quite bizarre."

"We'll get to the bottom of it, Dad," Suzi said.

"Right," Roop added. "If time is broken, we'll fix it." He peered into the window of the cooker. "I hope *this* isn't broken. It's going pretty slow."

Ned took a deep breath and pulled his communicator off his utility belt. "That reminds me."

"Oh, yeah," said Ernie, nudging him. "Ned just about blew up my school today. I wasn't sure we were going to make it out alive."

Ned smiled at his friend. It was true. His communicator had bageled them big-time. "It hasn't been right since we got blasted on Planet Wu. It needs to be rewired."

"Ah, Planet Wu!" Roop sighed exaggeratedly. "One of my favorite happy fun places!"

Suzi laughed. "We can fix your Neddy in the tech bay." Communicators were called Neddies after Ned, who had actually invented them.

Ernie made a face. "Planet Wu. Man, I miss one mission and I'm clueless. Fill me in again about your ride on the space shuttle and Zoa, the giant insect who talks into your brain, and blue-faced commandos and weird crystals and—"

KA-SHOOOM! Suddenly the *Tempus 5* rocked violently, as if it had been hit.

"Hey!" yelled Ned, bracing himself against the table. "What's going on?"

Sloop! The bulkhead flashed up and a Time Surfer ran in. She wore the green uniform of the *Tempus 5*'s flight crew. "Commander Naguchi, an unidentified vessel has just pulled out of hyperspace and is—"

KA-SHOOM! The ship rocked again, sending the Time Surfers stumbling to the floor.

"Bagel!" Roop exclaimed. "We're under attack!"

"Alert all battle stations! I'm going to the control deck!" cried Commander Naguchi. "Surfers, get ready to defend our ship!"

Suzi ran for the lockers on one wall and ripped them open. Inside were armored flight suits and high-tech utility belts. She began tossing the belts to the squad. "Whoever it is, they won't get us without a fight!"

Weee-ooop! An alarm whined through the ship as it quaked from another powerful blast.

"Unknown entities on board!" droned a voice over the communication system.

"We're being boarded!" yelled Ernie, grabbing two armored suits from Suzi and tossing one to Ned. "Fill me in later about your last mission. I think we've got a new one!"

KRIPPP! An awful grinding sound came from the forward section of the *Tempus 5*, sending shock waves through the ship.

"Umph!" Roop growled, sprawling headfirst across the table. A bowl of dried banana chips went flying.

Ned fell backward into one of the swivel seats. His communicator careened out across the large room as if he'd thrown it like a baseball. He lunged, trying to catch it before it smashed to the floor.

Suddenly everything began to slow down.

"B-B-B-B-B-But . . . ," Ned started. That was as far as he got. He saw Ernie, Suzi, Roop, and all the others in the galley slow down and hang mid-step in the air. The overhead lights flickered.

A strange hush blanketed the room.

"B-B-B—" Ned's brain seemed to slow down with everything else, but not as much.

Things moved, but incredibly slowly. It was as if time had wound down slower and slower and slower.

Extreme slow motion.

Then, *whoosh!*—the hatch opened with a flash.

And something rushed in.

Something not human.

CHAPTER
✳ 2 ✳

Worm . . .

That was the word that formed slowly in Ned's brain as the fat wet body with the thick head and small eyes squeezed through the hatch.

And then another squeezed in. And another.

"Grosssss!" Ned wanted to hide, or get out of the way so the things wouldn't slime him. But he was still moving in extreme slow motion, falling ever so slowly.

The wormlike creatures chugged upright along the floor, their bodies curved in an S.

Small clawlike hands at the ends of short stubby arms waved weapons at the Time Surfers.

The worms' weapons reminded Ned of ones

he'd seen in old science fiction books. Tubes and wild nozzles sprang out from the sides. Long silver barrels flared out into wide purple cones.

Clunky was the word Ned thought of.

But he couldn't say it. He couldn't say anything. He tried, but he knew it would take an hour before any sound came out.

Floo! Sloorp! Within moments, about twenty worms had chugged into the room. They yanked open lockers and overturned tables. They grabbed some blasters and some stunners, sniffed them, and tossed them away.

"Find shoot-shoot gun!" one of the creatures blurted out to the others, spraying spit from his big soft mouth as he said it.

Through the spray of dried banana chips that hung in midair, Ned saw Ernie inching his way downward. In a half an hour, he'd hit the floor. Suzi's hand was trying to move. It would be at least twenty minutes before her hand reached her utility belt.

Lost time! Yes, this was it. The worms had done something to slow time. But *they* were still in normal time. Weird. Very weird.

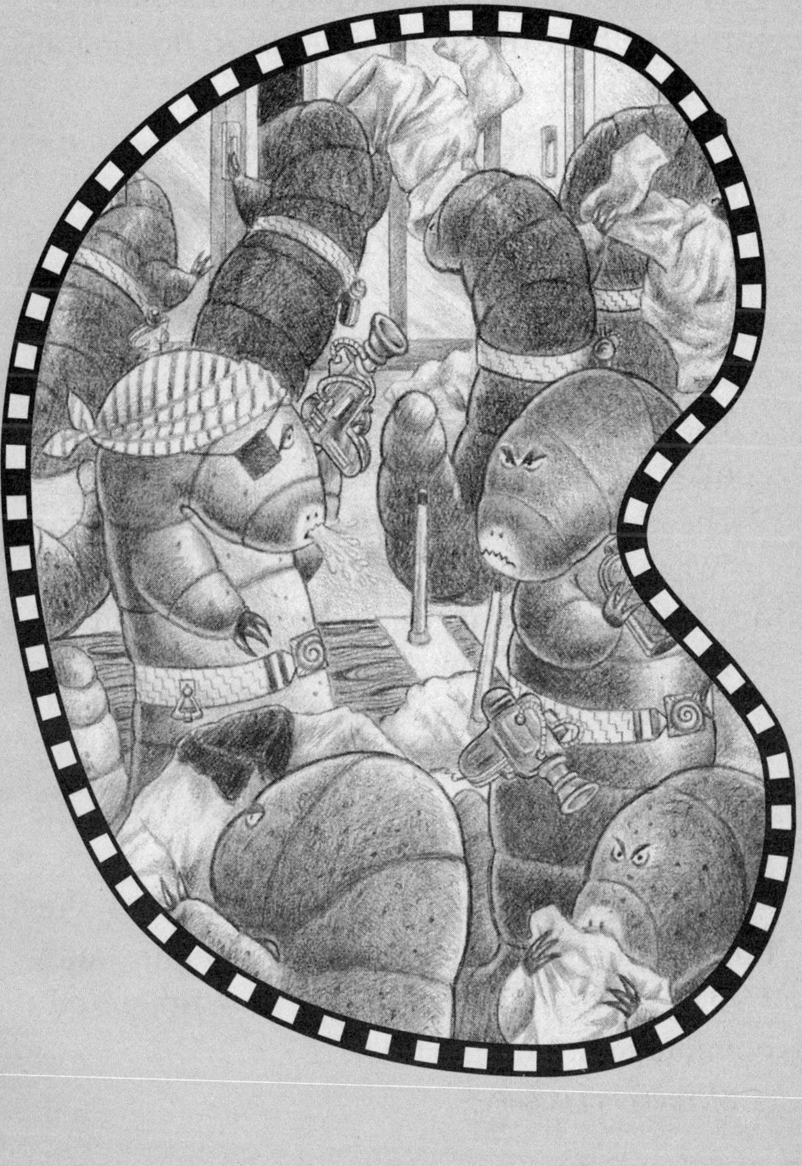

Then Ned caught sight of something out of the corner of his eye. Something black, floating an inch above the floor.

My communicator! he thought. *It's going to hit the floor! It'll probably go off again!*

"Ah!" snorted one of the worms. "Food in cooker! Mmm?"

"Take! Take!" blurted another worm close by, brandishing his clunky gun at the Surfers.

The first worm ripped open the door of the cooker and plunged his stubby arm in.

The cooker was very hot.

"Waaaah! Eoooogh!" the worm cried, yanking out his stubby arm. He jerked back from the cooker—and right into the dried banana chips that floated in the air, inches from his nose.

The chips startled him.

"Blaggggh!" the worm squealed. He fired at the chips with his big clunky weapon.

Ka-ploom! The worm's flare-barreled gun burst a fiery spray across the tables, instantly charring the tiny chips. At the same time, Ned's communicator hit the floor.

Skreeeeeeeeeeeee!

KA-VOOM! With a sudden loud explosion, the slowdown shattered and everything started to move at normal speed again.

Wham! Ned hit the table.

Wham! Ernie hit the floor.

"Blaghh! Time . . . back!" blubbered one of the worms, spitting everywhere. He fired his gun.

KA-PLOOM!

"Surfers, hit the dust!" yelled Roop. "Or *be* dust!"

"Ned, Ernie, over here!" cried Suzi. She slid across the floor and leaped with Roop behind an overturned table. Ned scrambled to Ernie and they headed for the table, sliding in back of it.

Two worms trained their guns on the Surfers while the others chugged around the room.

"These creatures are called the Feng," Suzi whispered breathlessly. "They're pirates. They board ships and steal whatever they can."

Ned made a face as he scanned the exits. "They seem sort of dumb."

Roop nodded, keeping low. "They're famous for that. But I never suspected they knew how to tamper with time. Good thing your Neddy cracked the slowdown, Ned, or we'd still be hanging out."

Ernie pulled out his stunner. "It screeched just like it did in school this morning."

"Right," Ned agreed. "Only here it went off the same time as the worm fired his spray gun."

Several of the pirates were tossing food and equipment into huge sacks over their backs.

"Control deck, then go!" one of them barked at the others. "We late! She be mad-mad!"

"She?" Ned repeated. "Mad-mad?"

The creatures squeezed back out of the cafeteria, still waving their clunky guns at the Surfers. An instant later, the Surfers were alone.

"They're heading for the control deck!" cried Suzi, jumping up from behind the table. She looked at Ned and the others. "My dad's up there. We have to help."

"We're on the job!" said Roop.

The Surfers yanked on their armored suits and raced down the corridor.

Right into the middle of something bad.

Ka-ploom! A fiery spray flashed across the corridor from the left. Another shot—*ka-ploom!*— ricocheted off the floor from their right.

"Cross fire!" Roop cried out, pulling Ernie to the floor just as a blast hit a hatch door behind them. "The Feng are shooting at each other!"

"You're right," said Ernie. "They are dumb!"

"Doom sandwich!" muttered Ned as another atom spray whizzed by. "Not my favorite." He scanned their escape options. There were two hatches, one near and one down at the far end.

Suzi headed for the first one. "This hatch goes to the engine room. We'll be safe there."

Suddenly the corridor behind them filled with shapes. Large shapes. Wormy shapes.

"No, let's take the other one," Ned said. "The worm dudes move slow. It'll buy more time!" He rushed past the first hatch and tore down to the end of the hall. Then he stopped. "Uh-oh."

"That did not sound like a good uh-oh," Roop said, racing with the others after Ned.

Ned frowned. "Well, what I thought was an escape hatch isn't a hatch at all." He pointed.

Before them was a jagged hole in the side of the freighter. On the other side was the Feng's boarding tube. The entry hole from their ship into the *Tempus 5*.

"Small ones!" one of the worms blurted out, spotting the Surfers. "Fry them! Hot! Hot!"

The kids were trapped. In seconds they'd be fried like those charred banana chips.

Ned wished he could turn back the clock and take that other corridor. But his Neddy was still acting weird. He was stuck in the here and now. And neither looked too good.

PLOOM! A shot exploded inches behind the Surfers.

"Is that an invitation?" said Suzi.

"I guess so!" said Ned, diving through the jagged opening into the Feng pirate vessel. He nearly slipped. "Whoa! The floor is covered with slime. Yuck!"

"Keep moving," cried Ernie. "We need a place to hide fast. Those worm dudes are coming!"

Ned slid ahead of the others. Then a blast of warm air whipped into his face from a vent above them. "The ventilation system!"

"I can see why they need one," Roop said, holding his nose. "Suzi, I'll boost you up."

Up near the ceiling, Suzi yanked off the vent cover and peered into a square hole. "Spacious!"

When the Feng chugged back into their ship's boarding tube, the Surfers were looking down at them through a ceiling grate, holding their breath.

"Small ones gone!" grunted one worm, swinging his gun around. "Cannot fry! Too bad!"

The worm troop slouched forward, their bags heavy with stolen equipment and food.

"Whew!" Ned gasped, letting his breath out. "Now let's get out of their ship before they—"

VROOOM! The Feng ship powered up and jerked away sharply from the *Tempus 5*. The whine of the engines filled the boarding tube.

"No!" yelled Roop. "This is not our *riiiiide*!"

The giant Feng vessel shot away from the *Tempus 5* and into deep space.

CHAPTER
✳ 3 ✳

Usually Ned loved feeling a ship go into fast forward. Not this time.

"Guys, we're stowaways," Ernie mumbled.

Ned thought about that for a while. "On the bright side, it's better than being prisoners."

Suzi nodded. "So let's try to keep from being captured. If we follow these vent shafts, maybe we can find an escape pod."

"And get back to the *Tempus* before the Feng enter hyperspace," Roop added.

The four Surfers began to crawl quietly and slowly through the square metal shaft toward the center of the ship.

Ned looked back at Ernie. He could tell they

were both thinking the same thing. *How did we end up here?* A couple of light-years away from Earth, on an enemy ship filled with chubby worm guys called Feng pirates?

The day had started out normal. It was Monday of the second week of the new year at Lakewood School. Just before his bus came, Ned had run upstairs to grab his communicator from its hiding place.

Errrk! His bedroom closet had squeaked open and Ernie had stepped out. "Hi, Ned! Let's have lunch in the cafeteria today. In your old school. Just like we used to?"

"I can't go to Newton Falls," Ned said. "My bus'll be here in five nanoseconds!"

Ernie made a face. "You'll be back in time. Remember, with timeholes we can have two whole lifetimes of fun."

Ned couldn't argue with that. It was what he had told Ernie way back when he'd first discovered timeholes. Now, Ernie just stood there grinning.

"Well, okay, for a few minutes." Ned grabbed his communicator and leaped into the timehole.

They emerged at the same moment from a timehole a thousand miles away.

"Wow!" Ned climbed out from under a stairwell in Ernie's school. "The school smells exactly the same as it did when I went here!"

"Schools always smell the same," Ernie said with a smirk. "It's a law, I think."

They headed toward the cafeteria. Ned heard the familiar lunchtime sounds of screaming and yelling. "I feel at home already."

Ernie nodded. "One thing that's new is Ms. Fanort, the lunch monitor. She hates noise. She wants everybody to eat quietly."

Ned chuckled. "As if that could ever happen."

When they walked up to the cafeteria doors, the noise hit them like a big fist. Two hundred kids were talking at the same time. And since that made it noisy, they all had to talk more and more loudly to be heard. Ned loved it.

In the middle of it all was Ms. Fanort, dressed in a brown suit. She was trying to get herself noticed. It wasn't working.

"I want to—" she started. "I want to be able to hear—" she tried again. "I should be able to—"

"It's sad, really," said Ned.

Suddenly Ms. Fanort stood up on a table and glared down at the students. *"I want silence—or you'll all get detention!"*

All the kids in the cafeteria went silent. That was when Ned accidentally dropped his communicator.

It went off. It was loud.

SKREEEEEEEEEEEEEE!

"Okay! Detention for everyone!" Ms. Fanort shrieked.

All the kids turned to the door and pointed.

"Oops!" Ned whispered. He began to tiptoe backward out of the cafeteria, as if he expected time to just back up and let him disappear.

It didn't work.

"Him!" yelled one of the kids. "He made the noise! He gave us detention! Get him!"

"Uh-oh!" cried Ernie. "Let's get out of here!"

Ned and Ernie had run for the stairwell, two hundred students chasing them down the hall.

Whoosh! Whoosh! The two Time Surfers leaped into the stairwell and into the future with only nanoseconds to spare.

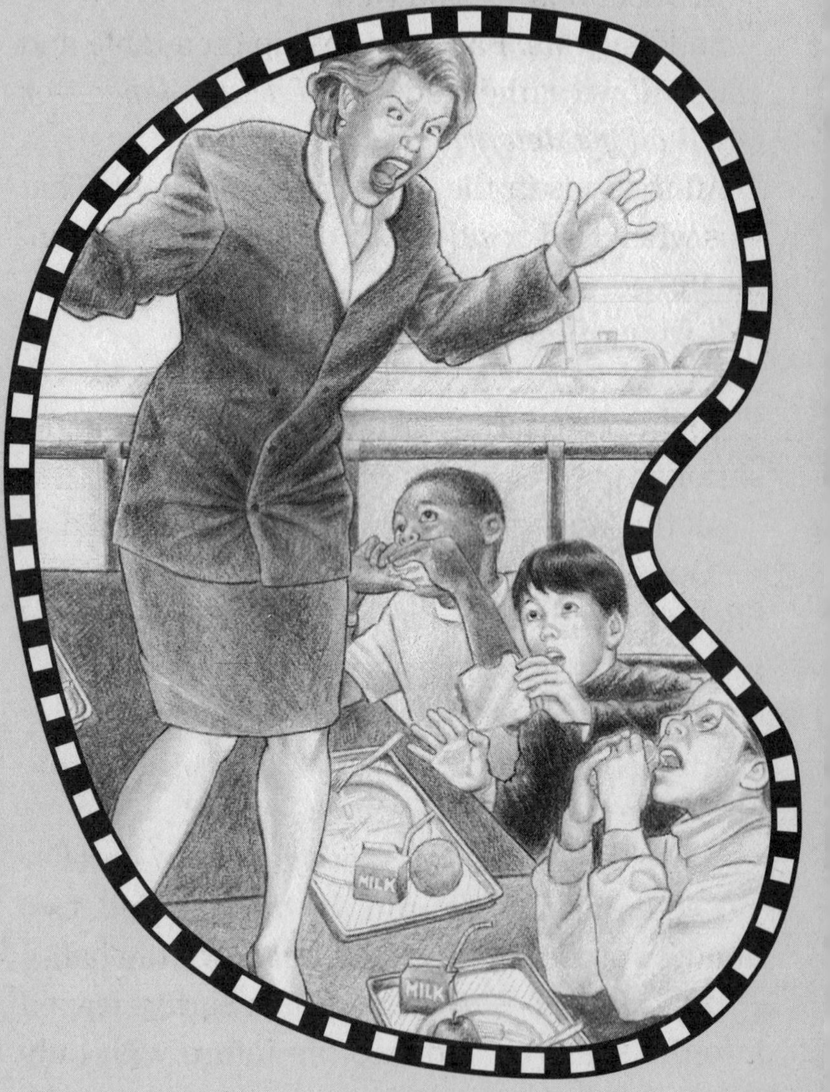
MILK
MILK

"Well," Ernie said, crawling along the air vent behind Ned. "At least we got out of there."

"Yeah," Ned muttered. "And right into here."

"Quiet, you two!" whispered Suzi. "There's something going on ahead." She crept up to another grate and peered down. Ned moved next to her.

The room below was the control deck of the Feng ship. There was a semicircular panel with large knobs and buttons on it. The screen of a large monitor glowed with the stars and planets the ship was moving through.

Slouched in giant chairs in front of the panel were two Feng pirates. Ned guessed the fatter one was the ship's captain. They were talking to someone Ned couldn't see, spraying spit each time they opened their mouths.

"No good food!" the captain worm said, waving his arms around angrily. "Blagh! Need more food! Mmm? More food?"

"I guess they didn't like the stuff on the *Tempus 5*," Ned whispered.

"We find more ships, we take more food?" asked the other. "Mmm? Food? More?"

Then came the answer. Ned nearly froze with fear when he heard it. It wasn't *what* the answer was, but *how* it came.

No! The time has come to begin our journey.

The answer wasn't spoken. The words—as silent as thought—penetrated Ned's brain directly, without sound. Instantly. Telepathically.

It sent a shiver through Ned, making his blood run icy cold. "Zoa!" he exclaimed.

Suzi clutched Ned's arm. "She can't be alive!"

Zoa. The dronth. Ned gasped as she moved into view.

Ernie tapped Ned on the arm. "You said she was almost dead the last time you saw her!"

That was true. The seven-foot-tall, hard-shelled creature had been seriously wounded. And her fortress on Planet Wu had been in flames, stormed by an army of blue-faced commandos called Talaks.

Ned shrugged. "I don't know. Maybe she formed a new shell or something?"

"Like cicadas do," Suzi offered.

Sure, thought Ned. Those little shells, like thin

brown plastic. He and Ernie used to find them in their backyards. Zoa had formed a new shell.

"Blagh!" blurted out the second worm, quivering in his chair. "Warp is good. We steal. We take. We find more guns! More food!"

Zoa twitched a little. *You blubbery fools. You see food. I see a new universe.*

"Lots food! Universe of food!" exploded the Feng captain again, shoving his stubby arm into a barrel next to the throne. He pulled it out and licked the goo dripping off it.

"I'm gonna be sick," said Ernie, rolling his eyes. He pulled back from the grate.

"Guys, this is not good." Ned groaned. "What is Zoa doing on this ship? With the Feng?"

Zoa moved jerkily across the control room, reminding Ned of stop-action animation. She towered over the Feng like an angry teacher.

Set course for your pathetic planet!

The Feng worms blustered, they spat, they waved their stubby arms all over, but finally they nodded and leaned over the panel. The ship bucked and entered hyperspace.

Zoa stalked around the room on her powerful legs.

"She gives me the creeps," whispered Roop. "She's like some kind of weird green skeleton."

"With incredible mental powers," Suzi added.

I shall return to the era when the dronth numbered in the billions, Zoa thought.

Ned doubted that the Feng understood Zoa. But they did what she wanted.

WHOOM! The ship shook once.

"We come!" said the captain, jiggling around in his seat. "Planet! Home!"

"We're going to land soon," Suzi whispered, looking at her friends. "Get ready to move."

Ned looked down at the giant monitor on the control panel below. The big brown planet dominating the screen was getting bigger and browner by the second. His heart beat faster. He checked his stunner clip. Fully recharged.

He was ready.

They were all ready.

But for what?

CHAPTER
✳ 4 ✳

Ka-thooom!

The main hatchway of the giant Feng ship closed with a resounding boom as the last worm pirate disembarked.

"Okay, guys, the ship is empty now," Roop whispered. "We can sneak out of here."

"And into what?" said Suzi, pulling aside the vent grate and dropping into the control room.

The large monitor above the control panel showed Zoa and the Feng entering a gate in a wall on the edge of a muddy field. They disappeared into one of the many giant brown cone-shaped structures inside the wall.

"We're in a city," said Ned. "A brown city."

"It's all dirt," Roop whispered. "This has to be the Feng's home planet. Worms love dirt, right?"

Roop was right. Two minutes later the Surfers were crouching under a giant wing of the arc-shaped Feng ship. They scanned the city clustered behind the wall for signs of movement.

"This is so weird," said Ernie. "It's like, "Where did you go today, son?' Oh, Planet Mud, Mom."

Chug! Splort! Sounds echoed across the field.

"Feng!" gasped Ned, pointing at a small troop of worms coming out from the main gate of the city. The Surfers scurried around to the rear of the Feng vessel and drew their stunners.

The worms roared over in a little car with a wagon on the back and stopped at the ship.

"Oh, let me guess," whispered Ernie. "These guys are the luggage crew?"

A giant port opened on the side of the ship. The Feng pulled sacks of stolen equipment and food from the opening and loaded them into the little wagon. When they were finished, the port closed and the worms drove the car back through the city gates.

"We need a ship we can fly home," said Suzi,

scanning the wall. "Maybe once upon a time, the Feng stole something like a surfie. Let's go see."

"I like the flying home part," said Roop. "I don't like the "let's go' part. You mean . . . into the Feng city?"

Suzi smiled. "Is this a mission or is this a mission?"

Roop chewed his lip and pretended to think about it. "Okay, but we'd better stay hidden. I don't think humans exactly fit in here."

The four Time Surfers crept cautiously across the field and into the city. The streets, which were no more than winding ditches of mud, were deserted. Conelike structures rose up all around them.

Suddenly the street ahead of them was alive with small slimy creatures, slithering in the mud.

"Whoa! Feng mice!" cried Roop, leaping back. "I hope there's another path we can take."

"Don't let these things get to you," said Ned as the mice scattered. "Think ship. Think escape. Think *home*."

Ten minutes later the kids eased up to a wall surrounding the central cone.

Beyond the large mud tower Ned noticed a walled area piled high with rusted junk. The luggage wagon pulled in and the Feng dumped the equipment from the *Tempus 5*.

"That's their junkyard," Ned said. At the back of the walled area was a shape. The rough shape of a flying ship.

"We can fly that one," Suzi said, studying the outline. "It's not too different from a surfie."

"The only entrance to the junkyard is from inside the cone," Ned said quietly. "We'll have to go through the cone to get to it."

The four kids looked at each other, took deep breaths, nodded, and entered the cone.

Inside the giant mound of mud, tunnels twisted off through the main hallway. Rough, round holes in the walls opened into mud-caked rooms.

As the Surfers crept along, they heard chattering from one of the rooms up ahead. They stepped carefully up to the entry hole.

Where is the crystal? The words came from inside the room, burning into their brains.

"Zoa!" Suzi gasped, pulling back instantly. "I don't think we want to go in there."

"Wait," Ned whispered. "We need to find out what she's up to." He peeked in. Though the hole was small, the room was large, its ceiling stretching up thirty feet or more.

Zoa towered over dozens of Feng. They were blubbering as they watched her.

In a tube of sizzling green light was something blue. A humanlike form, but with bright blue skin covering an oversized head. The head had no features. Its face was like stretched blue clay.

"That's a Talak commando," Ned whispered. "Like the kind that attacked Zoa on Planet Wu. She must have captured him."

The tall insect bent her triangular pod head toward the blue man. He twisted in the tube of light.

"Mind probe!" gasped Suzi. "The Talak won't be able to hide any secrets from her."

Still nothing? To the next level of probe, then! Zoa said. *Where is the crystal hidden?*

The Talak shot up to the top of the tube and

hung there, twisting silently. The Feng blubbered and wagged their arms. Ned guessed they were laughing at the Talak up in the air.

You may laugh! Zoa snarled, turning away. *The Feng mind isn't even worth probing!*

The Feng chattered and squealed some more. They thought that was just as funny.

The blue Talak gave up no secrets. Zoa lowered him to the floor.

Two Feng pirates wheeled a complicated device into the room.

"The prism!" Ned whispered. "The neutronic prism Zoa stole from the space shuttle!"

A worm removed a small, shiny object from the prism and held it up. "Crystal good!"

That's nothing more than the tiniest fragment of the photon crystal, Zoa said.

"Crystal good!" the Feng captain blustered. "It slow time good. We steal more food!"

The crystal can do more than slow time, Zoa said. *It can . . . reverse time. When I find it, I shall return time to the era when the dronth numbered in the billions. To the era when . . .*

Zoa's brown pod head turned suddenly toward the doorway. *I sense . . . intruders!*

"Blagh! Small ones!" One fat worm pirate fumbled with the giant gun he held.

PLOOM! He blasted a chunk of mud from the wall by the entry hole. Dirt sprayed everywhere.

"That's our cue to bolt!" said Roop, scrambling to his feet. "Everybody this way!"

But around the corner the Surfers ran into another band of chugging Feng.

"Back the other way!" Ned shouted. They shot down a side tunnel, the worms slouching right behind them. The tunnel ended in a large round room. The Surfers leaped into the entry hole at top speed and slid across the muddy floor.

"Uh-oh, dead end!" Ned jumped to his feet. "There's got to be a way out. Maybe a crack in the wall."

"No way," said Roop. "This mud is as hard as cement." He swung his stunner around to the entry hole. "We're trapped, and the worm guys are coming. Things don't look good, people."

"We have definitely entered level two of this

game," Ernie said. "We'll be captured, our minds will be probed, and Zoa will hang us up to dry!"

Ned felt something rumbling under his feet. Something thumping harder and harder.

"We've got to stop her from getting that crystal," said Suzi. "Turning back time to dronth rule could destroy the galaxy!"

"Wait!" Ned slid over to the far wall. "I hear something clunking behind this wall. But it's not the Feng. They chug. Who's coming?"

"Not who," said Suzi, her ear to the wall. "It's a what. Some kind of machine. And it's coming fast!"

"Another doom sandwich!" shouted Ernie, turning to face the entrance.

WHAM! The back wall exploded just as two large Feng worms squeezed into the entry hole. Chunks of dirt flew out across the room.

The walls crumbled.

Something big punched through the mud. It was a fist.

A giant iron fist.

CHAPTER ✳ 5 ✳

FOONG! FOONG! Bursts of laser fire exploded from the iron fist, destroying the entry hole in a fiery barrage.

"Eooogh!" screeched the head Feng pirate. He and his squad scurried back down the tunnel.

FOONG! The fist blasted again. The Time Surfers leaped back as a giant figure burst through the crumbling wall and into the fiery light.

"It's a robot!" Ernie yelled when he saw the big metal shape. "A killer robot!"

Ned's eyes went wide as the hulking shape strode closer, finally emerging from the cloud of dust. "That's no killer robot. That's Chip!"

Chip's wide, round barrel of a head swiveled

toward the kids. "Sorry I'm late." He lifted a giant fist. *Clank!* He gave everyone a snap wave.

Ned instantly recalled the first time he'd seen the powerful robot. He'd blasted to their rescue on the sinister planet known as M-Star 47.

Something moved in the darkness behind Chip. The Surfers crouched, ready to fire.

"Hey! You wouldn't stun an old friend, would you?" said a voice from the darkness.

Roop moved closer. "Ace?"

A teenage boy stepped out next to Chip. "None other, Time Surfers!" It was Ace Zonn, Chip's human partner. He grinned at the Surfers.

"Boy, you two just love big entrances, don't you?" said Suzi, breaking into a smile.

"You bet," Ace said, nodding at the entry hole. "But right now we need a big exit. It won't be long before the worm boys chug back in here."

Chip's thick leg struts turned. "This way." He powered back through the wall, crumbling it.

"You heard the robot," Ace said, jumping after him through the debris. The Surfers followed.

And just in time. The room behind them soon

filled with Feng. "Small ones! Bang-bang them!" they blubbered. But none of their shots hit the mark.

The Surfers bolted after Chip and Ace through one muddy tunnel after another.

"Keep going," Ace urged them. "The Feng captured us when we were making a courier run in the Laan star system. If we can get to my ship, we can hyperspace out of here."

Suzi shot a look at Ace. "That was *your* sawtooth we saw. They raided our ship, too."

"Galactic scavengers," snarled Ace. "I just hope they haven't broken up my rig for parts!"

"Grrr!" droned Chip. He strode quickly through the tunnels, the computer lights on his chest blinking. Then he stopped at the base of one tunnel. There was light at the end. His head swiveled right, then left. "Zoa. Feng, too."

Ned smelled fresh air. The field was out at the end of the tunnel. So was any hope of escape.

Ace turned to the Time Surfers. "They know we're here. We have to get out to that junkyard blasting with all we've got!"

Ace, Chip, and the Time Surfers stepped toward the light at the same time as a dozen fat Feng squeezed into the tunnel behind them.

"Uh-oh." Ned gulped. "Level three action."

Suddenly something small scurried across the tunnel floor between the Surfers and the Feng.

"More Feng mice!" cried Ernie.

"BLEEEGH! Tiny! Tiny! Shoot!" screamed a Feng, jumping back. He slid on his own slime, fell into the other worms, and dropped his gun.

In that instant, Ned saw his chance. "Surfers, run!" He grabbed the Feng's weapon, lifted it to his shoulder, and fired.

KA-PLOOM! A jolt of energy exploded into the mass of Feng, hurling Ned to the ground. The pirates reeled back, chittering wildly.

"Everybody grab on to Chip!" Ace shouted. "He's not just a robot, he's a rocket! We can fly over to my ship!"

Roop, Ace, Ernie, and Suzi surged out of the tunnel and grabbed the handles on Chip's back.

"Wait for me!" yelped Ned, struggling to get to his feet.

Vrrrrr! Chip's twin leg rockets began to glow.

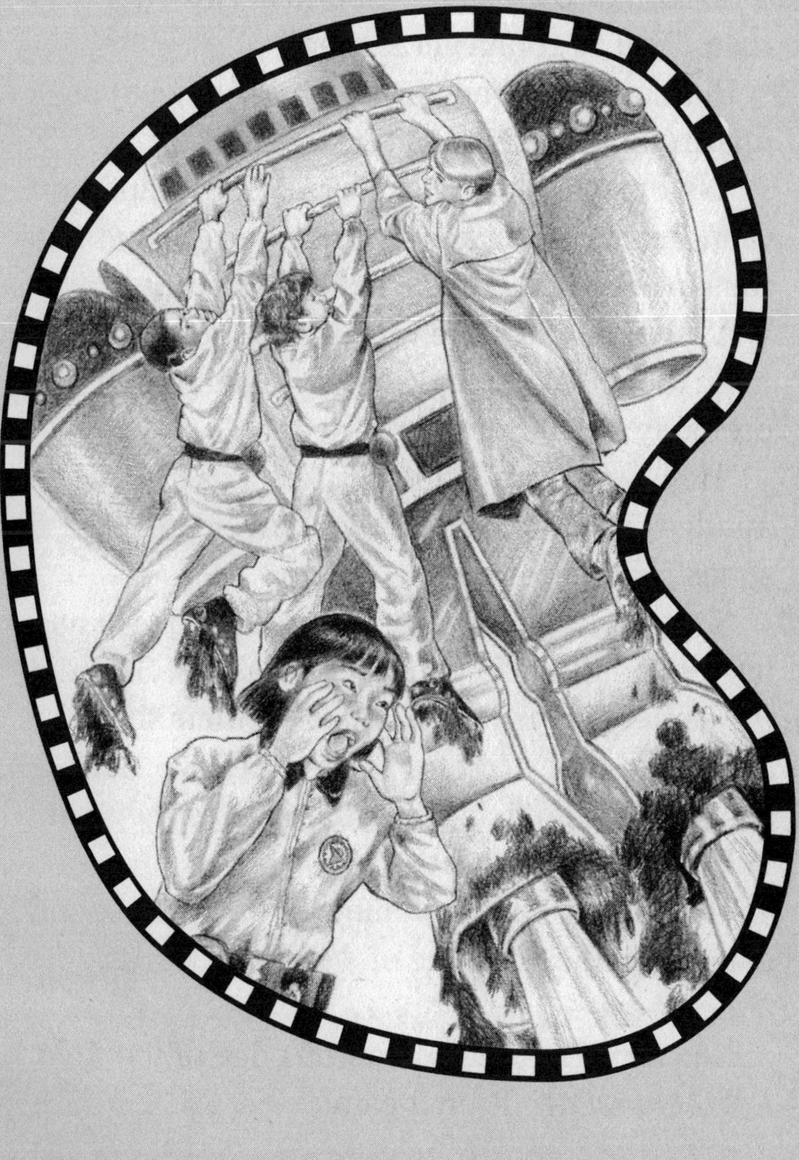

"Ned, get over here!" shouted Ernie as they rose. "You're gonna get sizzled!"

But dozens of Feng pirates had chugged back up through the tunnel after Ned.

"Ned needs help!" Suzi cried. She jumped off Chip just as he inched up from the ground and rose over the field toward the sawtooth.

A moment later she was sliding over to Ned.

He looked at her and smiled. "Thanks, but you probably shouldn't have done that."

"Hey, what are Time Surfers for?" Suzi reminded him. "Besides, we have our speed shoes!"

"I totally forgot!" said Ned. He leaned over and hit the small buttons on his sneakers. Suzi did the same. Tiny rockets flamed on their shoes.

Amid a hail of Feng blasts, the two Surfers shot across the field, spraying mud as they ran.

PLOOM! KA-PLOOM!

The barrage was deafening. But another sound came over the booming of weapons. Words.

Let them—

Ned turned to see Zoa at the edge of the field. *Let them what?* Then it came.

Kkkkzzzz! A blinding flash of light blazing across the field toward him and Suzi. It seemed to come from Zoa. From her great pod head.

"Umph!" Ned felt as if he had been hit in the back. But he had to keep going. Then the light vanished.

Vooom! Chip landed next to Ace's sawtooth. He swiveled and pumped laser blasts into the advancing Feng until Ned and Suzi ran to safety.

"Thanks, Suzi!" Ned gasped when they reached the ship. He turned. Hundreds of Feng roared across the field, taking aim.

Then Zoa raised her arm.

"Ned, hop in!" cried Suzi, leaping into the cockpit with the others. Ned jumped in.

The Feng fussed. They splurted. They waved their stubby arms. But they didn't fire.

Why? Why? Ned grabbed hold of the seat as—

VOOOM! The sawtooth blew off the pad and corkscrewed up over the cone city into the air.

They hit hyperspace even before the mud planet had faded under the clouds below.

CHAPTER
✳ 6 ✳

"We're in the fast lane, kids!" Ace whooped, the force of their speed shoving him back in his pilot's seat. "We're warping so hot even Feng arc ships can't find us now. My sawtooth makes it easy!"

Ned glanced through one of the portals that lined the small cabin. The wing to his left was jagged, like a saw's blade, giving the ship its name.

Easy? Too easy.

Ned kept seeing Zoa's arm held high. Why hadn't she let the Feng fire? Why had she let the Surfers get away so easily? And what was that flash of light that had burst over them?

"We might see some action up ahead," Ace told the Surfers, tapping Chip's metal shoulder.

"Activating sensors," the robot droned. With a small connector tube, Chip linked directly to the sawtooth's astronavigation computer.

Suzi and Roop studied the control panel while Ernie gazed out at space.

"We can go anywhere now," Ace told his passengers. He leaned back in his seat. "Actually, I'm thinking about going to Earth. I hear it's nice there. And the worms don't carry atom guns."

"The insects are tiny, too," said Ernie.

"Yeah." Ace shook his head. "Zoa. That dronth is up to something big-time."

Right, thought Ned. *Big-time. Very big-time.* "Zoa wants to spin the galaxy down using the photon crystal," he said.

Suzi nodded. "Just a tiny piece of the crystal makes time slow down. The Feng used it on *Tempus 5*."

Roop looked at Ace. "And Zoa mind-probed a Talak guy to find out where the big crystal is."

Ace shook his head and made a face. Then he let out a long breath. "I don't know where the

43

crystal is," the teenage pilot said. "But I know someone who does."

Ned's mouth dropped open. "You do?"

"Grrr!" Chip droned as the ship wheezed and buzzed through one star system after another.

Ace looked at Chip. "Chip is one of three robots created by the Talaks to guard the crystal. The other two were destroyed when the Talaks wiped out the dronth in the asteroid wars."

"That's amazing!" Ned cried. "How did you guys meet?"

"Kandar Zonn rescued me," Chip droned.

"Kandar Zonn is my father," Ace explained. "Chip was my baby-sitter when I was growing up. Anyway, during one really mega asteroid battle, the crystal was broken. Zoa stole a tiny shard. Now she's working with the Feng."

Ned thought about Zoa's uplifted arm again.

"Why is Zoa with them?" asked Ernie. "I don't think it's for the company."

Ace smiled. "Because there are billions of them. She's the brain and they're the body. Controlling billions of anything makes for more power. And Zoa wants power."

Suzi nodded. "She needs them to fight the Talaks. And to get to the crystal."

Ace scanned the star-filled space in front of them. "Just before the wars ended, the Talaks captured Chip and erased what they thought was his memory. But I had already rewired him. What they erased was . . . something else."

"Grrr!" Chip droned.

"Hey, how many times do I have to say I'm sorry?" Ace pleaded to Chip.

"What did they erase?" Roop asked.

Ace leaned over to the Surfers and whispered, "His sense of humor!"

"GRRRR!" Chip growled, swiveling his head at Ace and scowling as well as a robot could.

Clink! Ace patted his metal friend's shoulder. "But now the time has come to dig into that memory of yours and tell us where the crystal is."

Chip was quiet for a while. Then he droned two words. "Doom Star."

"Doom Star?" Ernie repeated. "Why not Fun Star? Or Play Star? *Doom* Star? Is that a joke?"

"I do not joke!" Chip scowled sideways at Ace.

Ned tried to put the pieces together. Slowly it began to make sense. Zoa wanted to bring the dronth back. She'd use the neutronic prism she had stolen from the space shuttle. She'd find the photon crystal. And she'd turn back time.

They had all seen how just the smallest fragment slowed time to a near standstill. With the large crystal, Zoa could reverse time and destroy everything.

"We have no choice but to stop Zoa," Ned said to the others. "We need to change course—from Earth to Doom Star!"

"No," Chip droned. "No change!"

"Neddo's right. We have to!" said Roop.

Ace shot a look at the robot. Then he began to smile. "What my partner is saying is that we're already headed for Doom Star. I guess we always knew we'd have to stop Zoa. But we didn't know *who* was going to have to convince *who*!"

Ned smiled. "We're gonna stop Zoa cold!"

"Quite cold," said Chip, pulling back on the controls to prepare for normal space. "Doom Star is an ice planet."

VOOORM! The engines whined shrilly and the

ship bucked. But no sooner had the sawtooth emerged from hyperspace into normal space-time than, swift as light, two shapes streaked across the atmosphere toward them.

"Talak fighter drones," said Chip.

"Too late to turn back now," said Ace.

The sleek blue airships pulled up on each side.

Kkk! Static crackled out of the screen on the panel. "You have entered Talak airspace," a voice announced. "Destruction lasers are trained on your ship. Do not attempt to escape. You will land now." *Kkk!* The speaker went dead.

"Aren't the Talaks sort of good guys?" asked Roop, staring out from the side port.

"We're the good guys, Roop," Ace said. "The Talaks don't like anybody who isn't blue. But we've got to tell them about Zoa."

Ace dropped the manual controls and slumped back in his seat. The small ship dived toward the surface. Snow-swept and ice-bound, the great white planet loomed before them.

Ned looked around at his friends. He gave them all a snap wave. "Good luck to us," he said.

After all that had happened so far on this

mission, Ned had no idea what to expect next.

But as the sawtooth veered toward the icy surface of Doom Star, a prisoner of the fierce Talak command, Ned knew it would be dangerous.

CHAPTER
✳ 7 ✳

The twin Talak fighters flew the small ship toward a gleaming dome that spread for miles over a vast, shimmering city.

Outside the dome, the earth was covered with frozen snow. Icy wind buffeted the three ships as they descended.

"They gave Doom Star the right name," said Ernie. "It doesn't look like a happy place."

The top of the dome opened and the three ships coiled down to a disk-shaped sky port.

"That's some city!" Roop scanned the streets below. "And no mud!"

No mud. But lots of blue. The fighters were

blue, the buildings were blue, the streets were blue, and the people were blue.

The ships landed. When the sawtooth's hatches opened, they were surrounded by a troop of blue soldiers. Their faces were flat and featureless.

Ace leaned over to the Surfers. "Let me do the honors. I've seen a lot of holofilms." He faced the Talak captain. "We come in peace! Take us to your leader!"

The Talak captain clicked his blue heels and gestured at a blue tube elevator on the landing area.

Ace nodded. "Come on, guys. Stick together."

They descended in the tube elevator and followed the blue-faced guards down a long hallway. They marched into a huge high-ceilinged room where trumpets erupted in a fanfare.

"Welcome!" a big voice resounded. "I am Talak Three! Please enter our court!"

"This is cool," said Suzi. "Maybe we won't have to escape this time."

Roop brushed the Time Surfers emblem on his

uniform. "Some respect would be nice for a change."

Everything in the court was a dazzling blue, including the throne. Like the other Talaks, Talak Three had no features on his face. But below his neck was an opening.

It was from this opening that his voice boomed. "Welcome to Doom Star!"

Ned stepped forward. "Thank you, sir. We're Time Surfers. We've just come from another planet. A planet of mud, and we need—"

"Ah!" the blue leader interrupted. "The filthy planet of the Feng! Our planet is very neat. No mud. We keep our city as clean as we can. Cleaning passes the time between wars."

"Uh, yes, sir." Ned took a breath. "Well, you may have another war on your hands soon."

Talak Three tilted his large blue head in concern. "Please explain."

The Surfers told him what had happened on the Feng's mud planet—how Zoa had the neutronic prism and was searching for the photon crystal, planning to spin down time to when the dronth ruled the galaxy.

When Ned had finished, Talak Three seemed to think over what he'd said. "Did Zoa track you here?"

"No," said Ace. "We escaped the planet in hyperspace. She didn't send ships after us."

"That is very good," the blue leader said, a tone of relief coming from his speaking hole.

Roop leaned over to Ace and the others. "I think you were wrong about the Talaks. They seem pretty reasonable."

Then the blue leader turned to one of the commanders to his right. "Talak Nine, you reported Zoa was eliminated. That report was incorrect."

Talak Three suddenly moved his head. *Ssss!* A slight hissing sound came from Talak Nine. An instant later, Talak Nine was gone. In his place was a wisp of smoke.

Roop jerked back. "Uh, that part about being reasonable? I take it back."

Talak Three's chest opening spoke. "You found your way to Doom Star. You know where the crystal is hidden. As guardians of the crystal, we cannot allow you to leave here. Ever."

"Now I really take it back!" said Roop.

"It's like I said," Ace whispered. "The Talaks don't like anyone who isn't blue."

Talak Three nodded. A moment later the room thickened with blue commandos.

"Okay," Ace whispered. "I don't think we can take the blue guys one on one, but I'm not ready to set up house here, are you?"

Roop scanned the exits. "Definitely not."

"Great. Then we'll use your plan," Ace said.

Roop blinked. "Plan? I don't have a plan! But I bet, uh, Suzi does!"

Chip's arm flicked slightly toward Ned's utility belt. Ned looked down. The lights on his Neddy flashed for an instant, then stopped.

Everyone looked at Suzi expectantly. She made a face, shook her head, and pointed to Ernie. Ernie shrugged.

Talak Three boomed, "Any last words before you are taken away to our detention tubes?"

"Blaggggh!" came a squeal from the back of the giant court. It was a fat, wet wormy Feng pirate at the door. "Blagh!" he blurted out again. "Talaks! Lots!"

Instantly there were hundreds of Feng, charging through the back door and tracking thick mud on the shiny floors.

"F-F-F-F-F-F-FENG!" Talak Three stammered.

KA-PLOOM! ZANG! BOOOM! The court exploded with bursts of lasers and atom sprays.

"Cross fire!" Ned dived for the floor. "Again!"

"The doorway!" cried Suzi. "It's clear!"

Instinct took over. The four Surfers headed for a doorway to their left, ducking blasts.

"Find the crystal!" Chip droned to Ned as he and Ace were caught in the cross fire and scrambled away across the court through another exit.

BLAM! ZANG! The battle intensified and spread to the streets outside. The Surfers ducked and dodged their way through the Talak court.

When they rushed outside, the sky was dark from an air attack above. Dozens of Feng ships and Talak fighters fired at each other.

"How did the Feng find us?" Ned cried.

BLOOM! The air thundered all around them.

"Never mind that!" yelled Suzi. "We've got to get out of this city!"

Eeeeep! Ned's communicator sounded. He whipped it off his belt and looked at the display.

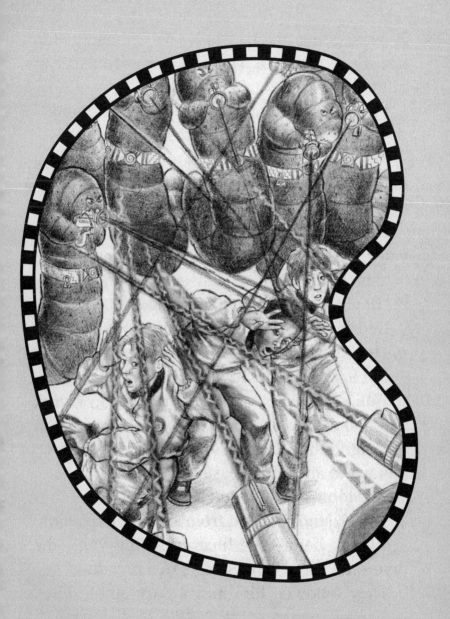

It was going wild. "It's . . . it's a map! Chip transferred his data. This will lead us to the crystal!"

BLAM! A Talak plane crashed behind them.

"Unless we get blown up first!" Roop cried.

The four Surfers dashed down a wide avenue, dodging explosions. Soon they came to the edge of the city. Beyond it lay a vast empire of ice.

Ned shivered. He shot a look at his communicator. "We have to go outside into the ice storm."

"And be frozen in a nanosecond!" cried Roop.

"Hey! Humans!" someone yelled out. "Stop!"

Ned jerked around suddenly, crouching and raising his stunner to zap a Talak or a Feng.

But it was neither. It was a human.

Well, sort of. He was old, with a shaggy beard, and about four feet tall. "You won't last long in the outdome!" he said. "I've got skins to keep you warm and sulfa beasts for travel!"

Ned looked at his friends. Suzi nodded.

The ground rumbled from another explosion.

"Come, before the blue ones find you!" the man said, waving the Surfers to a tiny door.

They followed him into a dark stable filled

56

with long-haired yellow animals. The beasts looked like a cross between camels and kangaroos.

"The blues are after you," said the small man, eyeing them from behind his shaggy beard.

"Yeah," said Ned, looking around at the large beasts. "The Talaks, the Feng, even a mad dronth. We're not making many friends today."

"Well, you just made one," the little man said. "Enemies of the blues are friends of mine. Take four beasts. When you're through with them, send them off. They'll find their way home."

Home. Ned felt a pang of pain. Would the Time Surfers ever see home again?

The sounds of battle closed in. Alarms wailed.

"Grab their manes!" the little man said.

"Thanks, mister!" cried Ned. "Surfers, let's go!" He grabbed a beast's stringy yellow fur.

Eooogh! The shaggy beast growled and burped as Ned climbed on. The small man gave the kids skins to cover their flight armor.

A moment later, four sulfas, carrying four Time Surfers, galloped out into the frozen wastes of the planet called Doom Star.

CHAPTER
✳ 8 ✳

Eooogh! Errgh! The sulfa beasts growled and plodded through the icy snow. Their long legs thumped into the deep drifts and whipped up a flurry of glistening crystals behind them.

Ned expected laser shots to blaze through the air at any moment. But there was only the wind.

He checked his Neddy every few minutes to stay on course. On course to find the crystal.

Ernie bounced up and down. Roop was hanging on to the shaggy mane with both hands. His teeth were gritted.

Ned was doing only a little better. After a few

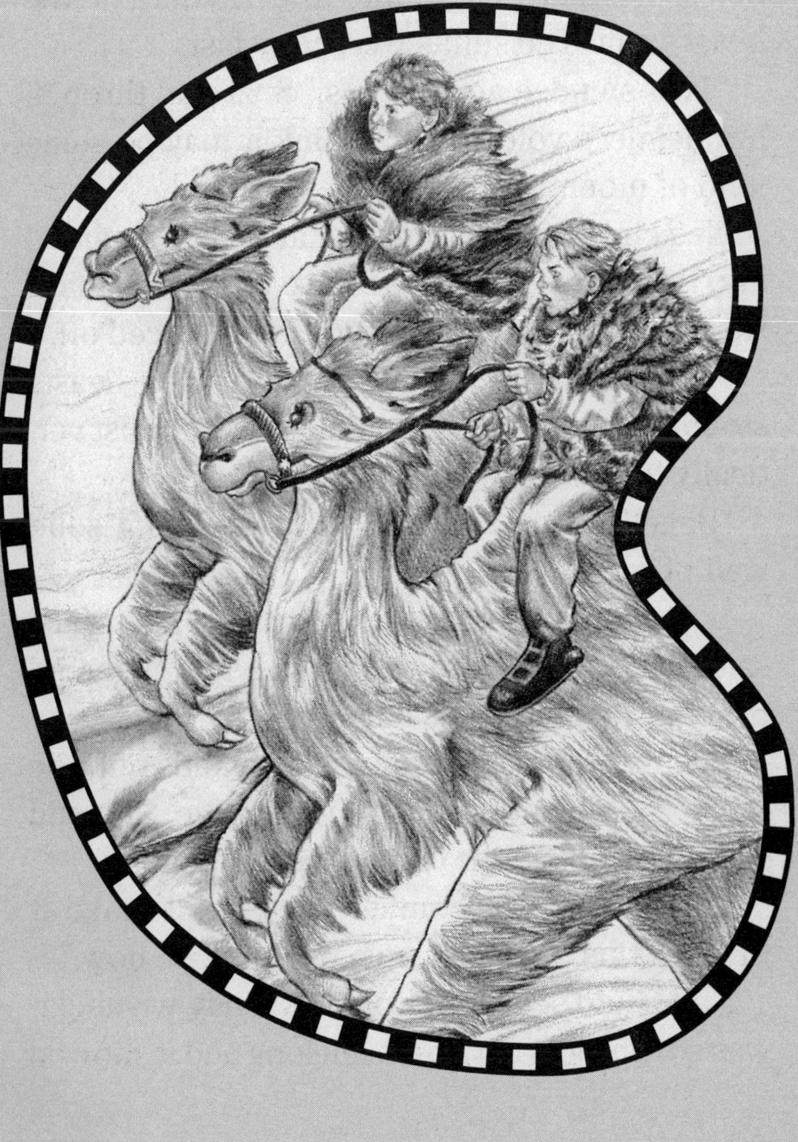

miles, he had gotten into the rhythm of the beast's gait. The sulfas were very fast.

"That smudge ahead of us," Suzi said through her helmet's voice link. "I think it may be some kind of mountain range."

Ned checked his communicator, then squinted into the distance. "Yes, we have to go over that." He tugged on the sulfa's mane, and it raced off.

An hour later the Surfers and their beasts stood at the foot of a mountain rising almost vertically from the icy surface.

"Bagel!" Roop snorted. "It looks like a solid wall of rock."

"I'm going to search for a way through," Suzi said. She and Ernie rode up to it while Ned read the small screen in his hand.

"I sure hope my communicator holds out," he told Roop, shivering under his fur wrap. "It could start screeching like crazy at any minute."

Roop managed a smile. "Hey, we'll make it through this. Besides, we must be close now."

Ned could see that Roop was really wishing it was so. The journey had been long and it showed no signs of being over. The cold was unrelenting. And the comfort of home seemed light-years away.

"There's an opening!" Ernie called from the mountain's face. "But we need to go in on foot!"

Roop and Ned galloped over and dismounted. The cave was too narrow for the sulfa beasts.

"Time to say goodbye!" said Suzi. She shooed the beasts away. They started back to the domed city.

"Remember," said Ned. "Our mission is to find that photon crystal before anyone else." He and Suzi pulled flashlights off their utility belts and led the way into the cave.

"Right, the crystal," Ernie mumbled as the cave wound down from the surface into darkness. "But what happens when we find it?"

Ned was struck by the question. He hadn't really thought that part all the way through. What Zoa wanted was too horrible to think about. She'd reverse time back to when the dronth ruled. And then change things so the dronth could take over the galaxy.

Worse than that, reversing time would wipe out everything that had happened in the past hundred million years.

Ned felt the forces tightening around them. Zoa, the Feng, the Talaks. They all wanted to stop the Surfers. Then it struck him. "This is a basic Time Surfer mission. Keep the galaxy healthy."

Suzi moved out of the tunnel and onto a ledge. The ledge hung out over a vast cavern. "Whoa! Is this the end of the line?"

Ned peered down. "Maybe the beginning."

The space below was miles deep and ended in mist. The cavern walls were smooth, sheer ice, pitted here and there with ledges and icy outcroppings. To Ned it looked more like the inside of a giant cylinder than a natural cavern.

An eerie greenish light tinted the hazy air deep below.

"Since there's no way up," said Roop, "I guess down is the way we go. Down into that weird light. Our powerclaws will help us."

The Surfers unlatched pistols from their belts. Ned and Ernie had never used them before.

"You fire this claw," said Suzi. "A line attached to the claw lowers you. The claw disconnects and rewinds for the next shot."

"Basic equipment," said Roop, throwing off his fur wrap. "Come on. It's a long way down."

Roop aimed at the ledge floor.

FLANG! The powerclaw sunk into the rock. Roop eased off the side, gripping his pistol with both hands. The line unwound, and he went down. Suzi shot her gun and followed him.

Ernie looked at Ned. "I don't really want to."

"I know what you mean. But think about it this way," Ned said. "The next time a teacher asks you what you've been doing, you'll have something to say."

Ernie nodded. "Assuming I'm still alive."

FLANG! FLANG! The two friends scaled down the icy cliff. The winds died away as they descended farther and farther from the summit.

One hour. Two hours.

After a while, the four Surfers stopped talking. They shot their powerclaws, descended, rewound, shot again.

With each noise echoing up from the cavern,

with each howl of the wind through the ice above, Ned felt as if *she* would soon appear. Zoa.

Somehow she had tracked them to Doom Star. Maybe she would track them here, too. Soon. But Ned had to steer away from those thoughts. They made him nervous. More nervous than he already was, scaling down ice cliffs, toward the weird, hazy light below.

One slip and—

"Help!" Ernie cried out. He slid swiftly down the surface, his powerclaw unhooking too soon from the ledge above.

"Ernie!" Ned shouted. Instantly he swung away from the cliff face and shot his own gun.

FLANG! The claw pierced a ledge, and the line went tight, strapping Ernie fast against the icy wall. He slid to a stop.

Ned quickly scrambled down to his friend as Roop and Suzi climbed up from below.

"What took you guys so long?" Ernie muttered, struggling up onto the ledge. "Man, this is rough!"

"It's meant to be," said Ned, recoiling his

powerclaw. "To protect the crystal the Talaks made this as hard as possible. We must be close."

The four Surfers descended once more. Their arms ached. Their fingers were nearly numb from the cold. But they kept going. They had to.

Ned glanced down at Suzi, her face set in determination, her hands searching for places to grip in the ice. Below her, Roop was already disappearing into the haze. The air around them was getting thicker and greener.

At last they set foot on the bottom. Solid ground. Ned planted his feet and breathed deeply for the first time in hours.

"Neddo, the map," said Roop, coiling his line up and holstering his powerclaw.

Ned pressed a button, and his communicator's screen came alive. "No way," he muttered. He turned and looked around him. The ground was a vast frozen sea, stretching for miles from one side of the cavern to the other.

He looked at the screen again. "This says it's right here. That we're standing on the spot where the crystal is supposed to be."

He looked between his feet. Just ice and snow. "Something's wrong. We're totally lost."

"You mean, after I nearly died up there?" said Ernie.

"After we all almost died!" Ned gasped. "It's not here! It's supposed to be here—"

KA-VOOM! A sudden explosion shook the cavern from above, sending tons of shattering ice and bursting rock booming down the walls.

Giant shadows swooped over them.

They were coming fast.

CHAPTER ✳ 9 ✳

"Arc ships!" cried Suzi. "The Feng!"

"They always know exactly where we are!" shouted Ernie. "How do they do that?"

"Jump behind the snowdrift!" cried Roop.

KA-WHOOM! The drift exploded into a mass of flame and shattering ice.

"Okay, not the snowdrift!" Roop shouted.

But when the snow and ice burst apart, something else happened, too. A crack sliced across the frozen ground, revealing something below them. Something circular and metallic.

"Ned, your communicator was right!" cried Suzi. "There's something under us. The crystal must be down there! It was here all along!"

KA-BOOM! BLAM! The Feng ships swooped at the four Surfers, blasting the cavern floor.

"We can't wait to be invited down below!" said Ned. "We've got to blast our way in!"

Suzi and Ned set their stunners to maximum and fired at the metal. *ZANG!* It burst open onto some kind of blue tunnel. A Talak tunnel.

"This must be the place!" said Ned.

Ernie frowned. "Shouldn't we scan for life-forms first? You know, blue life-forms?"

BLAAAM! The Feng ships fired at the kids.

Suzi made a face. "I think we better move it, or *we* won't even be life-forms!"

They jumped down through the blast hole and down into the blue tunnel. Ned could hear the Feng ships above them. They stopped their attack and came in for a landing. "Zoa's coming, I feel it," said Ned. "We've got to find that crystal fast."

They tore off down the tunnel, their steps echoing off the blue metal walls.

"It's incredible," Ernie said, running beside Roop. "The Talaks built this place to protect the crystal. And Chip used to be one of the guards."

"Yeah," Roop agreed. "That dude has some history. Too bad he can't get a joke."

The tunnels crisscrossed each other.

Suzi pulled up next to Ned. "It's a maze down here. The Talaks didn't want anyone to—" She held her hand up and everyone stopped. Leaning against the wall, she peered out into an intersecting tunnel. Then she straightened and moved ahead. The others followed her in.

Before them was an octagonal chamber.

"Holy smoke!" Ned gasped as he stepped into it. The walls were formed of shimmering metallic panels. The room hummed.

And there, on a pedestal in the center of the room, brilliant green light surrounding it, was the photon crystal.

"It's awesome!" Ned whispered.

The ground rumbled around them.

"You can feel its power," Roop said.

Suzi nodded slowly. "The air is . . . I don't know . . . filled with some kind of energy."

"Amazing," said Ernie. "This thing can turn back time. It can destroy everything we know."

Now that he'd seen the crystal, Ned could truly

believe what Ernie had said. The crystal was alive with power, pulsing from its center like a miniature sun. The display of light shimmering out through its facets was dazzling.

More rumbling came from above and shook the metallic room. Ned heard sounds echoing into the chamber from outside the tunnels.

"They're here!" Ernie shouted. "The Feng have broken in and they're coming down!" He whirled to face the entrance to the chamber.

Before he could say another word, dozens of Feng pirates had filled the tunnel.

"Blagh! Small ones!" their captain squealed, bursting into the chamber.

"Not so fast!" Roop yelled, jumping over with Ernie, their stunners set to maximum.

Suzi dashed back with Ned to the crystal.

"Go!" the captain spat. "Or we shoot-shoot!"

Ned knew it was now or never. He reached into the shimmering waves of light and grabbed the photon crystal. His friends surrounded him.

The crystal is mine! Give it to me!

The words pierced Ned's brain like a knife. He turned to see Zoa, her black eyes pulsing with

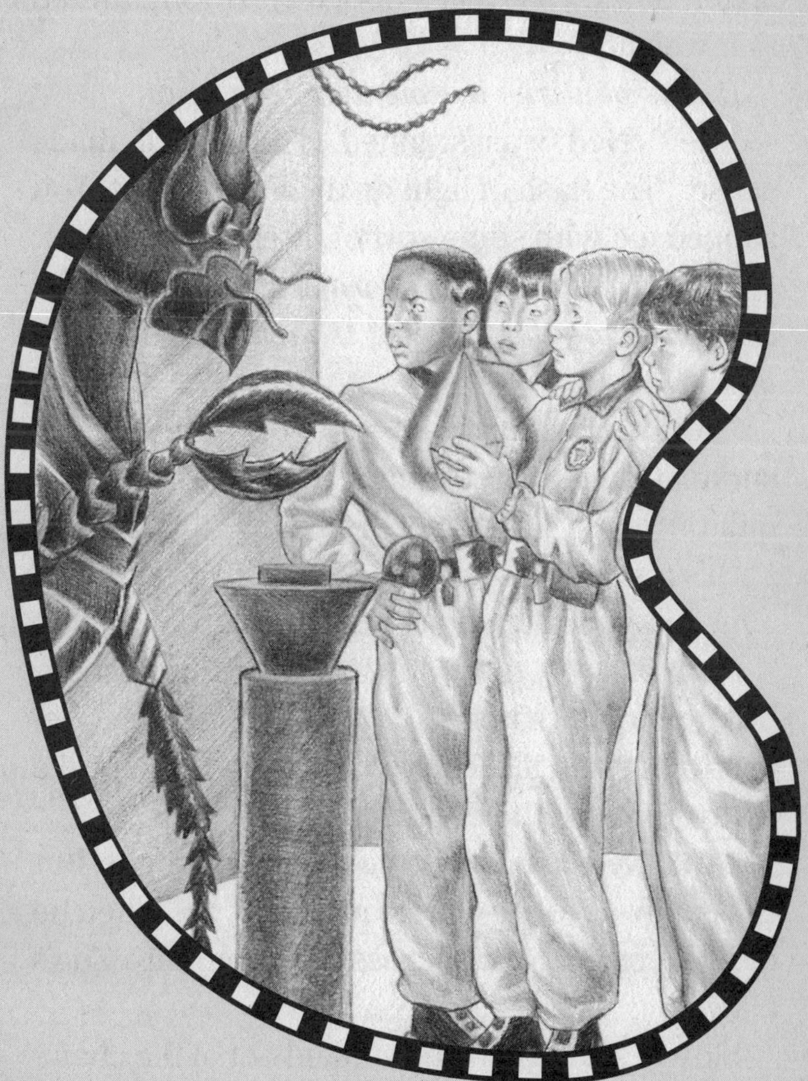

anger, in the chamber's doorway. He shuddered at the sight.

It was you who led me here, Zoa said.

"Me?" Ned was stunned. Then it all made sense. "The flash of light on the Feng planet! You zapped me with some sort of transmitter beam!"

I followed you every step of the way, Zoa said. *Now give me the crystal! It means nothing to you.*

"Nothing but survival," said Suzi fiercely. "The survival of every living thing in the past hundred million years! That's worth saving."

"It's a standoff, Zoa," said Roop. "My stunner's aimed at your big pod head. Let us go!"

No, it is you who will let go! At that instant, Zoa's pincers twitched at Ned and his hand began to burn as if the crystal was on fire. Sparks sprayed out of the crystal.

"No!" Ned cried out, trying to hold it tight. But the pain was too great. He had to let go. When he did, the crystal shot across the room into Zoa's claws.

Slowly she turned and stalked out of the chamber. Then her words came through. *Eliminate them.*

"Blagggh!" said one of the Feng, scowling and waving his big gun. "Splort! We shoot you! You gone!"

Eliminate them!

CHAPTER
✳ 10 ✳

The Feng chattered and massed together. Their captain squeezed out front. "Me splort small ones!"

Ernie edged back to Ned. "Uh, we could use a little help right about now," he said.

"A little help?" Roop repeated. "A small army might be nice!"

At that moment Ned remembered something. "Wait—a small army? Yes! How about an army small enough to fit in your pocket?"

Ned shoved his hand into his pocket and pulled out the small, flat cartridge of the holo-bloogball game. He hit a button on it and set the game on the floor, handing Ernie the controller.

"Hey, Feng!" Ned shouted. "I know how much you like little creatures! Ernie, do your stuff!"

Ernie's fingers blurred across the control pad as miniature versions of the four Surfers appeared on the floor. "Attack!" he cried, sending the small figures charging toward the Feng.

"BLEEEGH! Tiny! Tiny! Shoot! Shoot!" the Feng whined. They fell back in fear, all squeezing toward the door at the same time.

"Brilliant!" Roop cried.

"Everybody follow me!" Ned yelled. "Whoa— here goes something slimy!" Ned ran and dived over the thrashing mass of Feng as they tried to escape the tiny rushing figures.

Sloop! Ned slid over the top of them and out of the chamber. He leaped up and ran through the tunnels, back up to the cavern floor. The others followed right behind him.

"Got to stop Zoa before it's too late!" Suzi cried, scrambling out onto the icy ground. But it was already too late.

A squad of Feng were dragging the neutronic prism toward Zoa, who stood in the center of the cavern floor. The prism was larger than the last time Ned had seen it. It had been modified. To do maximum evil.

Now the galaxy will stop spinning.

Zoa inserted the photon crystal into a slot at the top of the prism. Instantly light burst from the crystal, illuminating the entire cavern.

"We're too late!" Suzi said.

Time will stop going forward. The dronth race shall return. Billions and billions of us.

KA-VOOM! A sudden stream of blue Talak fighter planes dived down from above, pumping fire at the cavern floor. The Feng scrambled to their ships. Moments later, they rose high to meet the Talak fighters.

But Zoa didn't seem to care. She stalked around the crystal, waiting for it to do its work.

Time will now . . . reverse.

Reverse. The word burned into Ned's brain.

But it wasn't because Zoa had said it. It was because in that instant, with only seconds left before time slowed and stopped, Ned knew what he had to do. "Stay here," he told his friends.

"What are you going to do?" Roop asked.

Ned pulled his communicator off his belt. "Remember that first warp event on *Tempus 5*? What broke the time slowdown was my Neddy going off at the same time as a Feng gun blast. I need to make that happen again."

Suzi shook her head. "But Zoa doesn't just want to slow time. She wants to reverse it."

"Exactly," Ned said. "If she does that, everything will happen again, only in reverse. That's why we have to stop her *before* we stop her."

Ernie gave his best friend a look. "Stop her *before* we stop her? You just lost me."

"Trust me," Ned said. Then he cracked a little smile. "Timing is everything!"

Zoa raised her pincers over her head. *The crystal's power! The dronth shall rise again!*

"Now!" Ned whispered to himself. Without another word, he dived out from behind a snowdrift and into the open. "Hey, worm dudes! Take your best shot!"

"Blagh!" squeaked the Feng, shooting a fiery blast at Ned at the same time as Ned threw his communicator to the ground.

KA-PLOOM-PLOOM! Feng guns exploded.

SKREEE! Ned's communicator squealed.

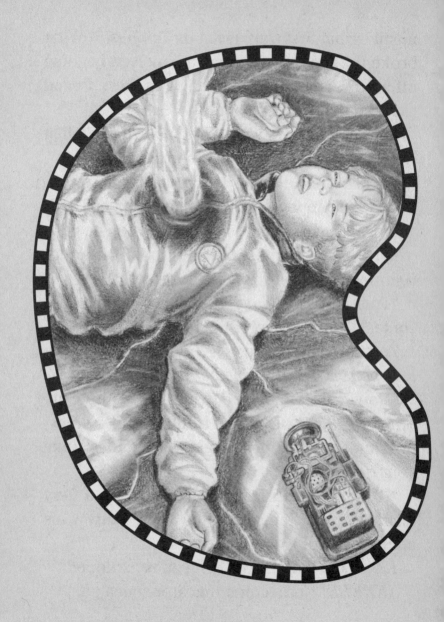

Wump! Ned felt the stinging hit from the Feng's volley. He was thrown to the ground. He landed slowly, crumpling into the snowdrifts. He saw his friends leaping up to help him.

Suddenly Ned felt time beginning to slow. Zoa's crystal! It had begun working! But was it too late for his plan to work?

The battle began to fade before Ned's eyes.

None of it seemed to matter anymore.

The sounds were getting softer . . . softer.

Ned's eyes flickered.

He had been badly hit.

Darkness overtook him.

CHAPTER
✳ 11 ✳

The atom spray had caught Ned full force.

As life seeped out of him, he could feel things slowing to a standstill. Through his half-closed eyes he caught sight of blue Talak fighters and Feng ships hanging in midbattle high above the cavern floor.

His three friends, Ernie Somers, Suzi Naguchi, and Roop Johnson, were frozen, half leaping up from behind the drift, their eyes focused on him.

Nice, to have so many good friends at the end.

Zoa, her pincers high in triumph, stood bathed in the crystal's powerful energy. She had won.

Ned's vision clouded. His eyes closed.

Then it began. Zoa's final victory.

Time stopped.

Then time began to spin backward.

And ever so slowly, Ned found his eyes flickering open. He saw Zoa, her pincers high, his friends unleaping themselves, going back down behind the drift.

And now he felt himself swooping back up from the ground, the atom spray of the Feng pulling out of him and shimmering back across the floor.

At that instant, with everything going backward like a video in rewind, the Feng's volley of shots at him and his communicator's screeching happened again. Only in reverse.

Eeeeeerks! went the communicator.

Moolp-moolp-moolp-ak! went the guns, their bursts being sucked back into the flared barrels.

And that was when it happened. A sudden, thunderous blast. Two jarring sounds coming together, exactly as they had on the *Tempus 5*.

KA-VOOOOOOOM! The air cracked with a flash of intense white light. The atom spray and the communicator screeching at precisely the same instant produced a tremendous explosion.

And the time reversal shattered.

The crystal shattered, too, into thousands of tiny fragments. Light sprayed across the cavern floor and disappeared into the glittering white ice and snow.

Everything began to move normally again.

"Zommo!" shouted Suzi, running to Ned and pulling him behind the snowdrift. "You did it!"

"You are incredible, dude!" Roop cried.

Ernie patted him on the back. "I thought you were dead for sure!"

Ned touched his chest where the blast had hit him. "I think I was, for sure!"

And you will be again!

Zoa, blown to the ground by the explosion, jerked up. She turned to Ned, a look of hate flashing in her large black eyes, and began to stalk toward him.

"We're still in hot water," said Suzi. "And we have no ride out of here."

The battle blazed above them. The Feng ships veered under the Talak fighters and fired.

KA-VOOM! VOOM! Two Talak ships went down, crashing into the snowdrifts and sending up a huge white wave.

Zoa stalked toward Ned as if none of this was happening. *You have destroyed my world! You will pay the ultimate price!*

That was when they saw it—a jagged-winged ship tearing through the battle above, dodging every blast!

BLAM! KA-BLAM!

"Ace!" shouted Roop. "And Chip! Zommo!"

"We've got our ride home!" cried Ned.

Ace and Chip flew their sawtooth flyer straight at Zoa, blasting the ground around her as if they were writing a paragraph with their lasers. It was incredible!

BLAM! BLAM! Ice exploded on every side of Zoa. She stopped. Then, shaking a pincer claw at Ned, she disappeared into her ship, burning angry thoughts at Ned and his friends. *I will be back!*

A moment later her ship shot away to the cavern summit. The Feng ships followed her, with the Talak fighters coiling up after them.

The sounds of battle soon died away, and the Surfers stood alone on the cavern floor.

Ned looked around at his friends and smiled. "Incredible. Did all that really happen?"

Ernie gave him a look. "Twice. I think."

Ace and Chip landed their ship in a snowdrift, and the hatch popped open. "Hey, dudes," Ace said, giving the kids a snap wave. "Sorry it took so long, but for a while it seemed like we were traveling backward."

"That was just the way you fly," Chip droned.

The Time Surfers climbed into the sawtooth. Then Ned blinked. "Hey, wait, was that a joke?"

"Yeah." Ace grinned at Ned. "When you guys escaped from the domed city, we weren't so lucky. The Talaks captured us and rewired Chip's circuitry to probe his memory. When they did, guess what Chip got back?"

Chip swiveled his head to the Surfers. "Memory? That reminds me of a story. A robot, an

84

android, and a cyborg were on their way to the fifth moon of Voongor, and the robot says—"

"See what I mean?" Ace said, starting up the ship's engines and pulling up from the cavern floor. "We're riding with Mr. Comedy. Talk about time slowing down. With jokes like these, our flight home is gonna seem endless!"

Fifty-eight stories, twenty-two riddles, and fourteen clank-clank jokes later, the Time Surfers arrived at Spider Base.

Ace and Chip decided to stay for a while. "Not only do kids rule," Ace said, "but the worms and insects are just the right size!"

"And the droids seem friendly," Chip added, striding off toward a group of laughing robots.

Ned stopped off in the tech bay to rewire his communicator so it wouldn't screech anymore. After that Ned and Ernie shot back through a shimmering timehole to the present.

FLONK! The stairwell at Newton Falls Elementary shuddered as Ned and Ernie spilled out onto the floor.

Ernie yawned. "It's only noon, and already I'm tired. Too bad that crystal exploded. I'd reverse time to last night and get more sleep."

"Reverse time?" Ned smiled over at his friend. "You know, that could actually be pretty zommo. We'd get to do the cool stuff all over again."

Ernie smiled too. "Unlimited lifetimes of fun. Total time surfing. Hey, it works for me!"

Then they heard footsteps down the hall. An army of teachers and students was running. "Get those two boys!" the crowd was yelling.

"Any chance we can reverse time now?" said Ernie, backing away. "We're in deep trouble."

Before Ned could answer—*whoosh!*—the timehole behind them blazed open. Two creatures bolted out of the blue hole. They had big red wings on their shoulders and purple spikes running down their arms.

"Don't laugh!" snapped Roop. "We're under cover!"

"As aliens from Zama Sector!" gasped Suzi. "You guys have time for another mission?"

"Another mission?" Ned shot a look at Ernie.

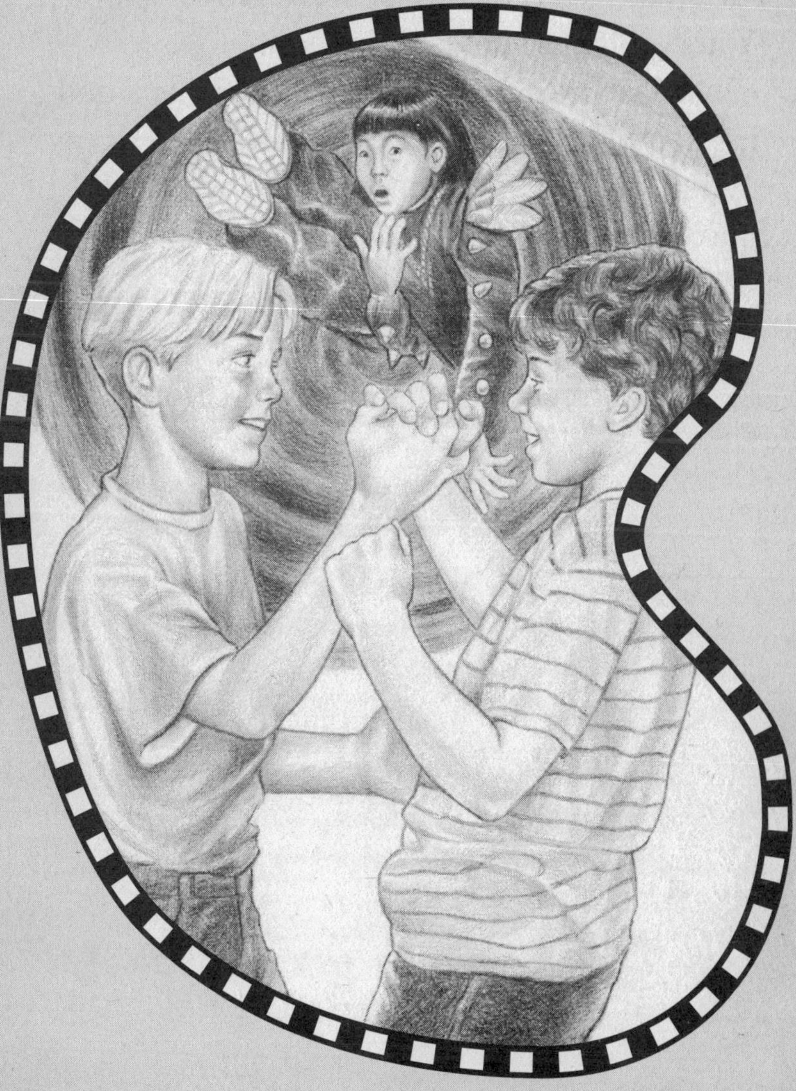

The sounds in the hallway were growing louder. "You bet! It sure beats detention!"

In a flash the four Time Surfers slid back under the stairwell.

And into the shimmering blue whirlwind of time.